"*Amazing Annabelle and the Fall Festival* by Linda Taylor is the second book in a series of books about a young girl with an abundance of spirit and determination. When Annabelle is chosen to run the craft booth at the Fall Festival, she is left to organize a committee of classmates who will be willing to work hard and bring her ideas to life. After an accident that makes Annabelle unable to run the committee, Annabelle worries if the people she has chosen are capable of finishing what was started.

"This book has a well thought out theme that children can relate to. The rich vocabulary used by the author enhances the text. It challenges the reader and allows the reader to naturally develop their vocabulary. Readers can easily relate to the characters in the story and will eagerly await the next book in the Amazing Annabelle series."

—*Nancy Woodward, Reading Specialist*

"The author, Linda Taylor, has captured the essence of Amazing Annabelle, a young inspiring African American student, who has supportive friends and family to help her creatively problem solve.

"She takes you through her day-to-day experiences in school with her friends and celebrate different seasons, holidays and cultural events. Amazing Annabelle is a realistic fictional series that all young readers should read and enjoy!"

—*Delfina Hennep, Speech Therapist*

Amazing Annabelle

AND THE FALL FESTIVAL

LINDA TAYLOR

ILLUSTRATED BY KYLE HORNE

a Sussman Education company

250 East 54th Street, P2
New York, NY 10022

www.lightswitchlearning.com

Lightswitch Learning is a trademark of Sussman Education, Inc.

Educators and Librarians, for a variety of teaching resources, visit
www.lightswitchlearning.com

ISBN: 978-1-94782902-2

Printed in Dominican Republic

To my countless

students—

Oh, how you've

inspired me!

Contents

The Fall Festival

An autumn breeze is blowing.
Excitement is in the air.
The Fall Festival is coming,
There's so much to do and prepare.

Annabelle's on the planning
committee.
Then an unfortunate injury
takes place.
She's on crutches and then—
Needs to call a friend.

Taking a back seat is
a change of pace.
Something Annabelle will
soon embrace.
She handles it with
kindness and grace.

1

FALL FESTIVAL MEETING

Today was a brisk fall day in October, the second month of school. So much was happening in Annabelle's life that she barely had any free time for herself. But that's how Annabelle liked things.

She was definitely a busy bee, full of energy and drive. She welcomed every activity and every task, no matter how big or small, and she always had high expectations.

Annabelle enjoyed doing amazing things that led to a greater purpose and made others happy. She was a people person who loved interesting conversations and activities with others. She wasn't your typical student.

Her mom would always tell her that if she wasn't such a small and youthful looking little girl, she could easily pass as a young adult. Annabelle loved just being a kid, and a very smart one at that. She was definitely going to make the most out of every situation and shine while doing whatever she put her mind to do.

Once, Annabelle had the crazy idea of having her very own Arts and Crafts Club right in her house! She asked her mom to take her to the store to buy construction paper, watercolor paints, and brushes. She created a large colorful poster that she placed in front of her house for all to see as advertisement for her club.

Then she created a schedule that listed the days they would meet and the specific activities they would do on each day. She even wrote down the supplies they would use and made illustrations on the schedule, which looked more like a fancy brochure.

When the first day of her club took place, she borrowed one of her dad's jazz CDs and played quiet music as her friends came to her house to begin class. She wanted to set the tone for creativity to happen.

She wanted everyone to paint a picture of something that made them feel good inside. It didn't matter what it was, just as long as they could tell a story that went with their creation.

She organized everything so well. She paid attention to every detail of each part of the club's first meeting, from the planning to the atmosphere.

Annabelle's idea for an Arts and

Crafts Club came from a children's show she saw on television once. She just changed things around a bit to suit her amazing creativity. Annabelle was definitely one of a kind, and the club was a major success.

Now it was October—the Fall Festival month at Melville School. It was a time for pumpkin picking and carving, hayrides, as well as trick-or-treating. As the school prepared for the Annual Fall Festival, there was a feeling of excitement in the air. All the students felt it.

In October, Mr. Jefferson, the principal, always chose the science theme, Changes in Fall, for the Curriculum Celebration throughout the building. Each class was responsible for doing a fall activity as well as making special decorations to display on the bulletin board outside their classrooms.

Annabelle was on the Fall Festival Youth Committee, which was led by Mrs. Griffin, the art teacher. Annabelle loved Mrs. Griffin because Annabelle loved art. She also liked how they both sometimes had the same natural hairstyles.

Annabelle was chosen to be part of this group because she was also a member of the Art Club that met after school every Wednesday. Kaitlyn, her best friend, was also a member of the Art Club as well as on the Youth Committee.

During the first meeting, Mrs. Griffin gave her introduction speech and then listened to all the new ideas from students on the committee. Darrell went first.

"I think it's time to dig into technology and create a fall pumpkin robot this year, and I can head up this very challenging project. You see, my dad works at Mercer Technologies and building robots is part of his job!" Darrell was super excited about his suggestion.

Mrs. Griffin really liked the sound of it. "That sounds great, Darrell. I'll follow up with your dad on that idea," she said.

Amber went next. "I would like to see a best costume contest. But in order to enter, the costume must be original, not store bought. Maybe all the kids could vote for the winner," Amber said.

"That's a good idea too." Mrs. Griffin nodded as she wrote all the ideas down on a clipboard.

"I think we should have a cool dance contest!" Kaitlyn said. Everyone seemed to love her idea.

Annabelle considered so many great ideas in her head that it was very hard to just think of one. So she just started speaking, hoping she wouldn't go on for too long.

"First, I think we should have a pumpkin and apple decorating center," she said. "The apples should be decorated with items such as marshmallows, raisins, and candy corn, so we can eat them afterwards. We can attach them with toothpicks.

"The pumpkins, on the other hand, could be decorated with markers, string, cotton balls, toothpicks, cereal, and all sorts of other items, since people can't eat them as is. Then, after they are done decorating, we could have a photo booth where the kids can take a picture with their decorated pumpkin or apple!"

She continued, "Others could also use the photo booth and take pictures with their friends and family to create special memories of this awesome Fall Festival!"

Annabelle could hardly control her excitement.

Mrs. Griffin looked at her with great delight. "Wow, I see you have really given this Fall Festival a lot of thought, Annabelle. I think *all* your ideas are great!" she said.

The other members all agreed with Mrs. Griffin and had good things to say about Annabelle's ideas. Mrs. Griffin ended the meeting with a few last words.

"All the ideas given today are totally great. The next step is to construct a game plan. I want everyone to think about how your idea will be completed. What will you need? Who will be involved? How will your plan be carried out successfully? I want everyone to write out the details for your ideas and present them at our next meeting," Mrs. Griffin said.

Annabelle left the meeting feeling happy about the next step. Kaitlyn was equally excited as they both walked to the late bus to go home.

"This is so perfect! I love all the ideas," Annabelle said.

"I'm going to start brushing up on

some new dance steps for the contest," Kaitlyn said.

"And I'm going to make a list of arts and crafts supplies I'll need as well as foods to decorate the apples. Hey, maybe you can come over tomorrow, and we can make a few samples!" Annabelle said.

"Only if you come over to my house and help me make up some dance steps and pick some good songs," Kaitlyn said.

Annabelle agreed. "That sounds like an amazing plan for the both of us! It's a deal."

2

DECISIONS AND ADVICE

When Annabelle arrived home, she kept thinking about the questions Mrs. Griffin asked at the end of the meeting. *Who will be involved? Who will help carry out this idea and bring it to life?* she thought.

"I will definitely have to organize a committee to work with me. But who on earth should I choose?" Annabelle said out loud.

Who has as much excitement as me? she wondered. She took out a little notebook and started jotting down some names of students she might choose. The first name she wrote down was Barry. He was a really good friend and lived on the same block as Annabelle.

"Barry could easily get to my house if an emergency committee meeting was called," she decided.

Annabelle put a big check by his name. The next name she wrote was Sally. Now, Sally used to be mean to her for the longest time, but they became friendly last month after working out some of their differences.

Maybe this would be a good opportunity for us to bond even more, Annabelle thought. *But then, what if things backfire and Sally starts being mean again?*

Annabelle wasn't totally sure about Sally, so she put a question mark by her name. The next name she put down was Vanessa. Even though Vanessa was kind of new to the school, Annabelle thought she had an adventurous spirit, plus she was very into sports. *But will her sports interfere with our after-school committee meeting?* Annabelle wondered. *Can I depend on Vanessa to carry her weight and be dependable and get things done?*

Just then, Annabelle's mom decided to check on her and find out what was on her mind.

"Hey honey, how was your day at school?" Mom asked.

"It was good. We had our first meeting for the Fall Festival, and now I have to round up some people to work with me on my big ideas."

"Wow, that sounds like a big undertaking. Are you sure you can handle it?" Mom asked.

"Mom, do you realize who you're talking to? This is just what I do. You know I always love a good challenge."

Annabelle's mom knew that statement was so true about her productive daughter. She continued to question Annabelle about the details of her project.

"So, I see you have to get some other students to help you pull things together. How is that going?" Mom asked.

Annabelle began to speak with a little uncertainty in her voice. "I just don't know who I can really trust at this point. I mean, a lot has to get done. I know I can count on myself and maybe Barry. But I'm just not too sure about the others," Annabelle said.

"Just remember, everyone is not going to be perfect or do things the same way you do. You must be open to their ideas and be understanding of their different opinions. You can't put the bar too high on what you expect," Mom wisely said.

Annabelle knew exactly what her

mom was talking about, and she definitely didn't want to scare off any possible committee members before she even got them involved.

"Thanks, Mom, for that advice. I know exactly what to do now."

"Well, I think my work here is done now," said Mom. "I know you're going to make some great choices. I can't wait to hear how things turn out. I'll see you later, sweetie." Mom kissed her gently on the head as she left her room.

Annabelle made a major decision right then as to what she would do. *I think I'll ask Barry, Sally, and Vanessa to be a part of this committee! I'll just have to accept what happens. I'll just remember that I'm a people person, and I can deal with anyone!*

Annabelle made plans to ask each person tomorrow during school at different times of the day.

Annabelle was thinking that she would ask Barry in the morning since he was the easiest one to get along with. Besides, she already knew him well, and she considered him to be a really good friend.

She was thinking that she'd ask Sally next, right before lunch. *Sally always seems to be happy at that time since it's her favorite time of the day.*

Finally, Annabelle would ask Vanessa right before Physical Education period. Vanessa loves sports, and Annabelle had the idea that just the thought of playing basketball would put Vanessa in a good mood.

Annabelle had everything worked out in her head. All she needed to do was stick to her plans. She was excited and eager for the next day.

"I'll pray tonight that everything will

turn out fine," Annabelle whispered to herself.

3

PLANS AND SURPRISES

The next day couldn't come quickly enough for Annabelle. She had made her plans, and now she was ready to carry them out. Annabelle spoke with Kaitlyn on the bus about her final decisions.

"Those sound like great plans, Annabelle, but always be ready for surprises," Kaitlyn said.

"What kind of surprises could there possibly be? I mean, I've really thought these plans out well," Annabelle said.

"Remember when Mrs. Mitchell was telling us about Murphy's Law that says anything that can go wrong, will go wrong," Kaitlyn said.

Annabelle thought that was a bunch of hogwash, which was a word she had heard her father use lots of times to describe something so unbelievably wrong.

"Well, I believe in having faith, and my faith says that even though things don't always line up with what you plan, they always work out for good."

"Well, alrighty then!" Kaitlyn said in a grown-up sounding voice. "You always have a great way of looking at things, darling." Annabelle began to laugh at Kaitlyn's voice as she joked around.

When all the students got off the buses, Annabelle immediately caught Vanessa's eye. She was walking into the school with Lila, a girl Annabelle really liked a lot. Annabelle walked up to both of them with a friendly greeting.

"Hey, Vanessa. Hey, Lila," Annabelle spoke quickly so as not to make them late for class.

"What are your thoughts on the Fall Festival coming up at the end of this month?" Annabelle asked.

"Well, I really hadn't given it any thought at all," said Vanessa.

"Me either," Lila said.

"Well, how would you two like the opportunity of helping me plan some arts and craft projects for the Fall Festival? We'd actually be working together as a group. What do you say? It's really going to be a lot of fun!" Annabelle said.

"It does sound really interesting," Lila said. "Okay, I'm in!" She was excited.

"Oh, that's great, Lila! We're going to have a great time, I guarantee it! How about you, Vanessa?" Annabelle asked.

"Well, I'm not sure. I just started playing for the basketball team, and I don't know if I'm going to have time to go to all the meetings," Vanessa said.

Annabelle already knew that this would be a concern for Vanessa. She was being very hopeful in asking Vanessa anyway. Annabelle knew she couldn't compete with basketball, especially when Vanessa was one of the star players. Therefore, Annabelle was very understanding and didn't get upset at all.

"No problem, Vanessa. I'll still fill you in on what's going on just in case you're able to participate on the day of the Festival," Annabelle replied.

"Okay, thanks," Vanessa said as she hurried off to class.

Annabelle quickly said a few last words to Lila before heading to class herself.

"So the first meeting will be tomorrow after school at my house," Annabelle said.

"Oh sure, I'll see you then!" Lila quickly responded as she went to her class.

What a pleasant surprise, Annabelle thought. Before today, she hadn't even considered Lila as a possibility for the committee.

As she walked towards the classroom, Annabelle wondered about what other surprises were in store for her.

The day was going great, as planned. Annabelle was about to put the next part of her plan into action. She noticed Sally getting her lunchbox to line up for the cafeteria. Annabelle immediately walked over to her and asked her the question of the day.

"Hey, Sally, you know, I was thinking. Would you like to be on a committee with me for the Fall Festival arts and crafts group? I know we would have a great time together organizing some cool activities," Annabelle asked.

Sally didn't even pause a second to give her short response.

"Not really. I'm not interested in that kind of stuff," she said quickly and then just kept moving along. Sally didn't even wait for a response back. So Annabelle called out after her, "Oh, okay then. Maybe next time or something!"

Annabelle felt a little uncomfortable about the whole scene that just took place. She wondered if Sally said no because she hadn't offered enough fun details, or was it just bad timing, or did she really *not* like arts and crafts. *But who doesn't like arts and crafts?* Annabelle wondered. *At least she wasn't mean about it.*

Annabelle was relieved. She concluded

that it just wasn't meant for Sally to be on the committee, and that was that.

As the day flew by, Annabelle remembered that she had one more person to ask, and that was Barry. She really hoped that Barry's response would be positive so they could have their first meeting as soon as possible. They were running out of time, and they had so much to do.

Annabelle saw Barry and Jake talking together at the end of class. Annabelle boldly approached Barry and interrupted his conversation with Jake.

"Excuse me, Jake. I just have to ask Barry a quick question. Would you like to be on a committee with me for the Fall Festival arts and craft group?" Annabelle spoke quickly.

"Sure, no problem. Are there going to be snacks at each meeting? You know your mom is so good with preparing snacks. Remember that time a bunch of us came over to your house and your mom gave us all those snacks? That was so awesome!" Barry said.

"Of course! We'll have tons of snacks! That's no problem at all," Annabelle assured him.

Jake spoke up unexpectedly. "Hey, that sounds like something I'd like to do too! Could I be a part of this little club?"

Annabelle looked very surprised and confused at the same time as she addressed Jake.

"Well, first of all, Jake, it's *not* a 'little club.' It's a committee of hard-working students who will be planning arts and crafts activities for the Fall Festival," Annabelle said.

"Great, where do I sign up?" Jake said in a cool voice.

"Well, actually you have to be chosen to be a part of this special group. But you can come to the meetings with Barry if you like," Annabelle said, a little uncertain of the offer she just made.

"Excellent! I can't wait until the first meeting!" Jake was on top of the world.

Annabelle would never reject anyone who wanted to join her Committee, even though she told Jake otherwise. She knew all too well how that felt, and everyone deserves an equal chance to be a part of whatever they choose.

"So, the first meeting will be tomorrow after school at my house. I'll see you both then."

"Oh, sure thing," Barry said.

"Absolutely," replied Jake.

Annabelle hurried to collect her things and get on the bus to go home. This was a day of changes and surprises, all wrapped up into one.

4

HOUSE MEETING

Annabelle had waited all day for school to end. She was so excited about the first committee meeting that was going to happen at her house.

Her mom had prepared a whole table of snacks for the committee members. Annabelle had to decide if she wanted them to eat first or have the meeting first and eat afterwards. Or they could eat while working, but that could complicate things with everyone talking with food in their mouths.

Annabelle heard the first doorbell ring from the den, and she quickly thought about asking everyone if they wanted to meet or eat first. And if there was a tie, then maybe they could play Rock-Paper-Scissors.

Lila was the first to arrive. Mrs. Copeland, Annabelle's mom, walked Lila into the den.

"Hey, Annabelle," said Lila. "I guess I'm the first one. I am such a stickler for time. I must be on time wherever I go. My mom says being on time always makes a good impression." Lila seemed to go on and on with endless chatter.

Annabelle actually didn't mind that Lila talked a lot. Lila reminded her of herself at times. Like Annabelle, Lila was cheerful, agreeable, diligent, delightful, dependable, hard-working, always on time, and the list could go on and on. They were going to get along just fine.

It was the two boys Annabelle was

worried about. Would they be able to pull their weight and carry out a task? This meeting wasn't going to be just fun and games and snacks. Annabelle really hoped Barry and Jake understood that.

Just then the doorbell rang again. Annabelle suspected it was one or both of them. Mrs. Copeland led both boys into the den.

"Hey, Annabelle, I hope we're not too late," Barry said.

"Yeah, that goes double for me," Jake added in his cool voice.

"Oh, no worries. We're all here now, so let's get right to work. We can all sit here around this table and get started." Annabelle took charge right away.

Jake happened to notice the snack table off to the side of the room.

"Hey, are those chocolate chip cookies

and juice boxes?" Jake asked, even though he already knew the answer.

"They sure are, Sherlock. We can't get anything past you, I guess," said Annabelle, surprised by her dig at Jake. It definitely slipped out by accident. She honestly didn't realize at first that she said it aloud instead of in a whisper. It was a good thing no one really noticed or said anything about her comment. Still, Annabelle attempted to make things better instantly by changing the subject.

"So, how about we eat some snacks first before we begin our meeting? Even better, why don't you just grab a plate of food and come on over to the table." Annabelle quickly motioned everyone to the snack table.

"Oh cool, don't mind if I do!" Jake said with a big grin.

After everyone got a plate filled with

snacks, they came over to the table and sat down, crunching and drinking away. Annabelle attempted to begin the meeting.

"As you know, the Fall Festival is in a few weeks, and I've been given the task of organizing the arts and crafts centers. I hope that each of you can be in charge of one station. All the materials will be provided by the P.T.A.," Annabelle said.

Barry and Jake kept right on feeding their faces but did stop every now and then to nod their heads. Annabelle noticed Lila had her notebook open, taking careful notes.

Lila was truly a girl after Annabelle's own heart. She sat attentively in her seat and even raised her hand to ask a question. Annabelle quickly called on Lila.

"Can you tell us what the various stations are," asked Lila, "and what our responsibilities will be in relation to each station?"

"That is a great question that I'm very happy to answer," Annabelle began. "The first station will be the Pumpkin Decorating Center. The second station is the Edible Apple Decorating Station, and the third station will be the Photo Booth.

"At each station, one of you will assist with passing out the supplies and helping the smaller kids complete their projects. At the Photo Booth, you'll just need to take pictures of each kid and their finished work of heart."

Barry was paying attention and quickly raised his hand to ask a question.

"Don't you mean work of 'art' instead of 'heart'?" Barry asked, very confused.

"Actually, since each child uses their creativity to make their final creation, I purposely said 'work of heart.' You see it takes heart to create such beautiful projects," Annabelle explained.

Barry seemed to look a little less confused now. Jake raised his hand to ask a question and Annabelle called on him.

"What is the P.T.A.?" Jake asked.

Lila quickly spoke up before Annabelle had a chance to respond.

"The P.T.A. stands for the Parent Teacher Association. Every school has one. They provide money to schools so they can do awesome activities like the Fall Festival!"

"Thank you for that explanation, Lila." Annabelle said with a smile.

"No problem. I was thinking that I could supervise the Pumpkin Decorating Station, if that's all right with everyone. I just love pumpkins!" Lila said with a grin.

"And I can seriously do the Photo Booth," said Jake. "I'm a techy kind of person, you know," he reminded everyone.

"Hey, I could help you out with that, dude!" Barry said. "We'll be the two cool photographers!" Jake and Barry really got a kick out of working together.

"I'll do the Edible Apple Decorating Station," said Annabelle, "and now everything is covered! I just want to thank you all for agreeing to be a part of this committee and this awesome Fall Festival." Annabelle was happy that the plans were going so well.

"Oh, no problem," said Jake. "I really enjoyed the snacks too! When is the next meeting? Are you going to have these snacks for the next meeting too?"

"Absolutely. Why not?" Annabelle let out a long sigh as she spoke.

It appeared that the snack idea really worked and maybe even helped fire up the guys. They didn't talk as much as they normally did because when they were feeding their faces.

But somehow, Annabelle was sure they were listening to every word, even if they didn't really act like they were. Annabelle realized that this meeting wasn't so bad after all. They really got a lot accomplished. Annabelle was quite pleased and felt really good inside.

5

MELTDOWN

The next morning on the bus, Annabelle and Kaitlyn sat next to each other as they normally do. Annabelle couldn't wait to tell Kaitlyn all the details about the first meeting, but she noticed that Kaitlyn wasn't her normal, cheerful self. Kaitlyn appeared to be really troubled about something and just stared out the window.

"Kaitlyn, what's wrong?" Annabelle asked, very concerned.

"Nothing is working well for me! I asked Julia and Dexter to help me plan the dance contest for the Fall Festival, and they were no help at all!" Kaitlyn sounded frustrated.

"Well, what happened? It couldn't have been that bad. It's just plans for a dance contest." Annabelle tried to make light of things.

"First of all, Dexter has two left feet and doesn't know any popular dance moves. Then, Julia has no rhythm and doesn't know any of the latest songs! I just don't know why they agreed to help in the first place when they knew they weren't good at dancing! What were they thinking?" Kaitlin really looked down.

"We got absolutely nothing accomplished at our first meeting," she went on, "except a lot of silliness and foolishness! What on earth am I going to do now?" It seemed as if Kaitlyn were going to explode!

Annabelle was wide-eyed and in complete shock. She had never seen Kaitlyn this upset before. Actually, she was beyond upset. Kaitlyn was very troubled, angry, and worried.

"Wow! I can't believe that. Maybe you can try to get some other kids to help you out and have another meeting," Annabelle suggested.

"What's the use? To be honest, I don't think I'm going to be able to put this dance contest together. I'm an official bookworm. I don't even listen to popular dance songs on the radio. I don't know any cool dance moves either! I don't know what I was thinking about when I volunteered to put together a dance contest." Kaitlyn was very down on herself.

"I really think you're looking at this all wrong," said Annabelle. "Kaitlyn, you don't have to know the latest dance moves or the latest songs to put together

a dance contest. All you need to do is hire a DJ that does this professionally!"

It was as if a lightbulb turned on in Kaitlyn's mind. She gave Annabelle a big smile and a sigh of relief.

"You're absolutely right! I was over thinking this whole thing! Getting a DJ would make my life so much easier. That's really who they use to get parties moving and grooving anyway," Kaitlyn remembered.

"Maybe you could ask the P.T.A. to buy some prizes and little gifts to give to all the dancers," Annabelle suggested.

Kaitlyn quickly took out her notebook and began writing Annabelle's ideas down.

"You're the best friend ever! What would I do without you? This is just one of the many reasons why we call you Amazing Annabelle!" Kaitlyn exclaimed.

Annabelle was so pleased that Kaitlyn's spirits were lifted and her immediate problems seemed solved.

Kaitlyn quickly changed the topic and inquired about Annabelle's plans.

"How did your first meeting go yesterday?" Kaitlyn asked.

Annabelle was excited to report her good news.

"It really went pretty well. I had my doubts at first, but everything came together for good. Jake and Barry were a little annoying at first when all they seemed to care about were the snacks my mom made. I almost lost my cool with Jake for a moment, but I held it together. The three stations have all been assigned and that's what really counts," Annabelle said proudly.

So, all went well with the first meeting. Annabelle couldn't wait to see what surprises were in store for the next one.

6

UNFORTUNATE INJURY

Once again Annabelle was excited for another amazing day of school. She had high hopes for the next committee meeting that was going to take place later after school.

Today was a physical education day, which Annabelle was never thrilled about. She loved running around and having a good time, but she wasn't a fan of organized sports. Mainly, she didn't like basketball. She just couldn't get the hang of the game, and she definitely wasn't good at it.

It just so happened that this particular

day was a basketball day. During physical education class, Annabelle was somehow chosen by Mr. Tucker to be a team captain along with Vanessa, who happened to be extremely good at basketball.

"Mr. Tucker, do I have to be the team captain? I'm really not that good at this," Annabelle asked with hope in her voice.

"Just try it, Annabelle, I'm sure you'll do a good job," said Mr. Tucker, making an effort to encourage her.

After each captain chose their players, they soon started a game. Of course, the captain couldn't sit on the bench, which is what Annabelle loved to do, so she had to join the rest and play the game. Although she felt as if she had two left feet, Annabelle went through the motions of the sport and tried as hard as she could to be a team player.

She was really messing up badly and

hardly ever touched the ball. Even when she was wide open, no one would pass the ball to her. However, Annabelle really didn't mind because if someone tossed the ball to her, she would be required to do something with it. So, her "ghost playing" went on until just about the end of class.

Then a horrible thing happened. As Annabelle was attempting to go for the basketball that somehow got very close to her, Vanessa was also going for the ball at the same time. Vanessa accidentally tripped Annabelle, who fell down hard on her knee.

Mr. Tucker immediately blew his whistle to stop the game and ran over to her. "Annabelle, are you all right? Don't try to move your knee now. Just lay still," Mr. Tucker instructed.

Annabelle was clutching her knee in

terrible pain as she tried to hold back her tears.

"Oh, it really hurts so badly!"

"I'm so sorry, Annabelle, I'm so sorry!" Vanessa felt so bad about what she'd accidentally done.

Mr. Tucker sent one of the girls to get the nurse quickly, and the gymnasium became very quiet. Many of the girls had tears in their eyes and felt bad for Annabelle.

Mr. Tucker sat down next to Annabelle to calm her down. "The nurse will be here any minute. You're going to be all right, Annabelle," Mr. Tucker said.

When the nurse arrived, she noticed the seriousness of Annabelle's injury and quickly got a wheelchair to roll her to her office. At this point, Annabelle could no longer hold back her tears.

Mrs. Copeland was called, and she came right away to pick up Annabelle at the school and take her to the doctor.

Word spread around the school quickly about what had happened to Annabelle during physical education class. Many students and teachers were very concerned about her.

No one was more concerned, however, than her best friend, Kaitlyn. The minute she got home, she told her mom about what happened. Kaitlyn's mom called the Copelands later that evening.

The news wasn't good. Annabelle would be out of school for a couple of days with a sprained knee. She would have to wear a knee brace and use crutches.

When Annabelle heard the news, she felt crushed. She had never missed a day of school in her entire life. How would she be able to get up the steps of the bus using crutches? More importantly, how could she continue to be on the Fall Festival Youth Committee and accomplish her ideas for the arts and crafts stations?

Annabelle definitely had a lot to think about, and she had two days off from school to put together another plan.

7

RECOVERY

While Annabelle was home, she felt miserable. While others may have enjoyed being waited on hand and foot, Annabelle didn't like it one bit.

She wanted to get out of bed first thing in the morning and practice walking on her crutches. She kept asking her mom and dad to help her move around with the crutches and knee brace so she could get lots of practice before she went back to school.

Yes, Annabelle was already thinking about going back to school. Annabelle was not one to sit around and do nothing.

Her mind had to be at work in some way, even if her body couldn't move as quickly as she wanted it to.

Annabelle kept all her school books, binders, and reading books right next to her bed on her night table at all times. She also had her special Fall Festival clipboard on her bed to remember the big tasks she had ahead of her.

Once her mom walked in the room as Annabelle was trying to use the crutches by herself.

"Annabelle," she said, "you must be careful! Remember what the doctor said. You're not fully healed yet. You can actually do more harm than good if you try to rush the process." Mom sounded very concerned.

"Mom, I can't stay in bed all day like this! I feel so useless!"

"Honey, healing takes time, and you

must exercise a little patience. You already did a lot of practice walking today, probably a little more than you should have. I know how you feel, but you must follow the doctor's orders. You shouldn't overdo it," Mom warned her.

"All right, all right," agreed Annabelle.

"But I just can't wait to get back to school and have another committee meeting here at the house. I really need to meet with everyone to discuss supplies and the layout of everything."

She picked up her clipboard and started going over the Fall Festival notes she had written down to discuss with the committee at the next meeting.

"Honey, are you sure you're going to be able to do all this extra work with the Fall Festival in your condition?" Mom asked. "You're not going to be able to get around like you used to for a while."

"I'll be able to get around just fine with this knee brace and these crutches," Annabelle said with a brave face.

"It's going to be hard enough getting back and forth to school each morning. A sprain like this can take a lot out of you. You may feel yourself getting more tired because you're using different muscles to move around," cautioned Mom.

"I'll make sure I eat a good breakfast each morning and take my vitamins. I'll also make sure I get to bed early every night," Annabelle said.

"You just may want to consider asking someone else to take over until you get your strength back fully. That's all I'm saying, honey. Remember the doctor said you have to take it easy."

Who could Annabelle possibly ask at such short notice? There was only one person and that would be Lila. But would she be able to do it? Lila was just like Annabelle in so many ways because she was a hard worker and very interested in completing a project with excellence. When they first met, Annabelle took a liking to her right away.

Annabelle started to agree with her

mom a bit about getting help with the Festival. Maybe she should take it easy for a while so she could be 100 percent for the actual Fall Festival in two weeks. Annabelle didn't want to miss that for the world. Maybe she could work in the background.

Annabelle's mom would always tell her that some of the brightest stars shine behind others, giving their light away. Annabelle decided that's exactly what she would do.

8

FRIENDLY VISIT

The next day after school, a lot of Annabelle's friends came by to visit her to see how she was doing. Annabelle was in good spirits and welcomed their surprise visit. Kaitlyn had arranged the whole thing with Mrs. Copeland's help. The balloons, fruit basket, and teddy bear they brought Annabelle really cheered her up.

Mrs. Copeland made a lot of snacks for all her friends so that it really felt like a Get-Well Party instead of a regular visit. Annabelle was so happy to see all her friends, especially Kaitlyn and the Fall Festival committee members.

Everyone stayed around for about thirty minutes, and then many started to leave. Annabelle really wanted to meet with the committee members briefly before they left. She finally assembled them all together by the snack table before she began talking about the Festival.

"Listen, I know you all are probably wondering what's going to happen with the Fall Festival committee meetings, the arts and craft ideas, and the photo booth station you all agreed to put together. I just want you to know that everything is still going on as planned."

Then Annabelle turned to Lila. "I really want to know if you could stand in and take my place, Lila. I truly believe you can bring everything together."

Annabelle thought Lila would be surprised by her invitation, but Lila gave her answer swiftly. "I would be honored, Annabelle, and thank you so much for believing in me. I won't let you down."

Annabelle thought her friend answered way too quickly. Maybe she just really wanted to take over and be the boss in the first place. Maybe Lila's plan all along was to be in charge.

Then Annabelle came back to her senses. She really liked Lila and knew she wasn't a bad person. Annabelle started to think about what her mom had said about giving others a chance to shine and let them be the light.

Barry and Jake continued to eat snacks, not caring one way or the other who was in charge.

"So does that mean we're going to start having meetings at Lila's house?" Barry asked.

"Are you going to have snacks too?" Jake asked.

Annabelle couldn't believe Jake's question and just let out a long sigh and shook her head.

Lila quickly put their minds at ease.

"We will definitely have the meetings at my house, and I will definitely arrange for snacks. That will be no problem at all."

"Thank you so much, Lila," said Annabelle. "I just wrote down a few suggestions and ideas of how things could go. But please feel free to change anything around. I'll definitely be there for the Fall Festival, but I don't know if I'll be able to do the Edible Apple Decorating Station." Lila could hear the sadness in her voice.

"Don't worry about anything, Annabelle," she said. "We'll take care of everything, right guys?" Lila looked over at Jake and Barry.

By this time, though, the boys had moved to the other side of the room and were getting ready to go home.

"I assure you, Annabelle, you have nothing to worry about. I have a good friend I can count on if Jake and Barry don't wind up helping much," Lila said with confidence.

Annabelle felt sad but hopeful at the same time. She was handing over the responsibility of her part in the Fall Festival to Lila, which she really didn't want to do. However, she knew in her heart that Lila could handle the challenge.

Now Annabelle could really concentrate on getting better and stronger with no outside distractions. This made her mom very happy. Maybe soon Annabelle would be happy about this decision as well.

9

WELCOME BACK!

Annabelle felt so relieved when she was finally cleared by the doctor to go back to school. It took four days instead of the two days they thought she would need for her sprain to improve. Annabelle had to go to physical therapy sessions daily, which helped strengthen her muscles.

A special teacher even came to her home to assist her in her studies. Annabelle was not about to fall behind in her school work. She was really getting used to the personal academic attention she was receiving for those four days, but today all of that would be coming to an end.

Annabelle was excited yet uneasy about returning to school. Thoughts raced through her mind a lot. *What if I don't use the crutches correctly and fall flat on my face? What if I get extremely tired after the first period of school? What if no one talks with me during recess because they want to play on the playground?*

While all the what-ifs clouded her mind, her mom called aloud to her, putting her thoughts on hold for a moment. It was time to go. Annabelle picked up her crutches and hobbled to her dad's car. He was going to drive her to school each morning until it was okay for her to take the bus again.

Annabelle's brother saw this as a great opportunity to be driven to school as well. Jason came running with his backpack in hand and yelled out, "Wait for me! I'm coming too!"

Annabelle was not happy. "Does Jason really have to be dropped off with me in the morning? I mean, he can still take the bus with all the other kids."

"Here's your backpack, Annabelle," said Jason. "I can help you carry it into school while you use your crutches. Is there anything else you need me to do?" Jason sounded sincere.

"Son, that's a really great thing to do for your big sis. I see you're really looking out for her," Dad commented.

Annabelle knew that Jason could be so fickle at times. His mom always said he was like a Dr. Jekyll and Mr. Hyde. Although Annabelle didn't know those old characters from so long ago, her mom explained that they were the same person with a good side and a bad side. One side was named Dr. Jekyll, and the other was named Mr. Hyde.

This morning Jason just happened to show his good side. Annabelle felt a little bad about not wanting him to ride with her to school.

"I guess you can come with us, Jason, and thanks for helping with my backpack," said Annabelle in a pleasant tone.

"No problem, Annabelle. I'll send you my bill at the end of the week." Jason gave a scary sounding laugh.

"Ha, ha, ha, right back to you. Now I see the real Jason coming out again," Annabelle said, a little bothered again.

But by this time Jason was already outside and in the back seat of Dad's car.

Annabelle didn't think any more about Jason because she had some nervous feelings as she rode quietly in the car.

When she arrived at school, she could hardly believe her eyes! Kaitlyn had arranged for some of her friends to meet Mr. Copeland's car in front of the school! Kaitlyn had made a banner that read, "Welcome Back, Annabelle!"

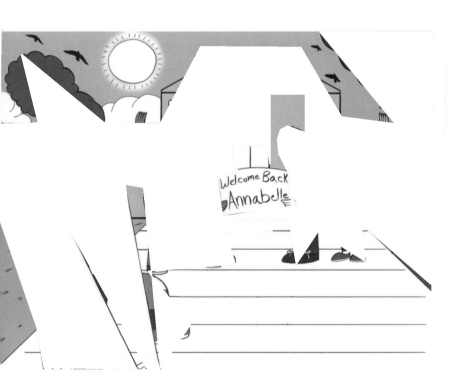

All her friends waved and cheered as she got out of the car. Annabelle was laughing and crying at the same time. Jason carried her backpack and joined in on all the fun. Annabelle's dad called to her as he started to drive away, "Have a great day, honey!"

Kaitlyn was the first to give her best friend a big heartfelt hug. "We're all so happy to see you back at school, Annabelle!"

Everyone joined in welcoming her and giving her hugs. The only thing Annabelle wished she could do was to hug everyone back, but she was limited since she was on crutches. Annabelle was comforted by all the attention and couldn't wait to get back into the swing of things.

She was very surprised to see Lila, Barry, and Jake in the crowd of well-wishers. Jake didn't even know her very well, but she guessed he came because he was a friend of Barry.

Annabelle wanted to ask so many questions about how the preparations were going for the Fall Festival, but since it was right around the corner, she didn't bother to ask. Besides, she had so much more on her mind about how her first day back in school was going to play out.

Kaitlyn and Barry walked with Annabelle to her classroom and held her crutches as she sat down at her seat. She received many smiles and hugs in her classroom as well. But the biggest came from her teacher, Mrs. Mitchell.

"I am so thankful to see you back in school, Annabelle," Mrs. Mitchell said. "As you can see, your class is very happy to see you back as well. I brought you a special apple today."

This was such a kind thing for Mrs. Mitchell's to do since Annabelle often brought an apple in for her.

"This is such a surprise, Mrs. Mitchell, thank you. I'm ready to get back to business as usual. I can't wait to do some work finally! Do we have a test today, because I'm ready for it!" Annabelle said, sounding very excited.

"Well, let's not get crazy now," said Barry. "There is definitely *no* test today. If anything, maybe Mrs. Mitchell will give us less work today and take it easy on us because of you, Annabelle. What do you say, Mrs. Mitchell?" Barry asked.

All the class joined in chanting, "Less work! Less work! Less work! Less work!"

But Mrs. Mitchell wasn't moved in the least and quickly put an end to the chant.

"Okay, class, let's settle down right now! And Barry, you get your first warning today for causing such a stir in class this morning," Mrs. Mitchell said.

"You can't blame a guy for trying," Barry said softly as he went to his seat.

Annabelle thought the morning went pretty okay, all things considered. She was able to catch up on some important assignments and even do fractions during math.

Now it was time for their Physical Education class. It was very obvious that Annabelle wouldn't be actually playing, so she had to sit on the sidelines in the gymnasium.

This place brought back unpleasant memories since it was the same place where she had been hurt. Annabelle decided to draw in her notebook to keep herself busy while her class played basketball.

Before the game began, Vanessa

walked over to Annabelle with a big smile on her face.

"It's really good to see you back at school, Annabelle," said Vanessa. "I felt so horrible about what happened. I'm so sorry for running into you like that. I just couldn't stop myself. I was just in the zone, diving for the ball, and the next thing I knew, you were on the ground grabbing your knee. It was just one of those freak accidents." Vanessa looked sad.

"No worries, Vanessa. These things just happen. It wasn't your fault. I really should have gotten out of the way. All is well. The doctor says my knee is healing, and I should be off these crutches in three weeks," Annabelle said.

"Oh, that's really great, Annabelle." Vanessa brightened up. "I'm really happy to hear that. So I guess I'll see you around," Vanessa said and ran off to join the game.

And that was it. Celebration and forgiveness were the order of the day. How great it was to be back in school!

10

FALL FESTIVAL FUN!

Today was the day Annabelle had waited for all month long—the Fall Festival. At school she could think of nothing else. The school day went by so fast as Annabelle daydreamed about it in class.

She wondered if all the committee members had planned well and were ready to set up the gymnasium right after school ended. Since the actual event didn't start until six o'clock, everyone had at least two and a half hours to make the gymnasium look perfect with fall decorations.

Once again, Annabelle wanted to ask Lila about the preparations but decided against doing that. She had to trust Lila to the very end. Lila had told her that everything was going to be fine. And since she was so much like Annabelle in so many ways, Annabelle believed her.

Once school was over for the day, Annabelle saw P.T.A. members starting to decorate the hallway leading to the gymnasium. She really wanted to stay after school with all the other youth committee members and help out, but she wouldn't be able to do much with her crutches. Besides, her mom was waiting outside in front of the school to pick her up.

Just then, Annabelle saw Lila headed toward the gymnasium with a big box of arts and craft supplies. Annabelle just couldn't resist the opportunity to speak, so she did.

"Hey, Lila! How's everything going?" Annabelle asked, hoping for a good report.

"We're just beginning to set up all the stations," Lila began. "The P.T.A. bought about one hundred small pumpkins! I was just going to start putting the tablecloths on the tables and set out all the arts and craft supplies. Why don't you come in and help us? I can make sure you're sitting all the time and not walking around on your crutches."

Annabelle couldn't believe what she was hearing. Was Lila really inviting her to help out? Even with her crutches? Annabelle didn't think of herself as being disabled and was sure she could still do simple tasks, even with her crutches. However, she thought that others might not see her quite as capable right now.

Annabelle quickly responded, "Of

course I would! Let me just go check with my mom. She's outside. I'll be right back!"

"I'll see you inside in a little while," Lila called back to her as she hurried into the gymnasium.

Annabelle couldn't get to her mom's car fast enough to tell her the good news. This was the happiest day of the month for Annabelle. Now she would get to participate in the Fall Festival and be part of the team.

"Mom, you're not going to believe what just happened. Lila just asked me if I could come in the gymnasium and help set up for the Fall Festival! Mom, I know what you're going to say. But I'm *not* going to overdo it! Lila says I can just sit down the whole time. I'll just be sorting stuff and opening and arranging art supplies on the table for the different stations. I won't even be standing up!" Annabelle leaned on her crutches with a glint of hope in her eye.

Her mom let out a long sigh before she responded. "Annabelle, you know what the doctor said. No strenuous movements." Mom sounded concerned.

"I'm not even going to move my knee, just my hands! Come on, Mom, please. You just have to trust me. I won't hurt myself. Please let me go. I've been waiting for this all month."

Mom looked into Annabelle's eyes and saw that her little girl really wanted to do this with all her heart, so finally she gave in.

"Okay, Annabelle, but you need to be super careful at all times. Jason and I should be at the school by five forty-five. If you need me for any reason, just call my cell phone," Mom said.

Annabelle tossed her backpack in the car and closed the door. "Thanks, Mom!" she called as she hurried inside.

When Annabelle got inside, she saw Kaitlyn setting up her table and putting little prizes on it to give to all the dancers. The DJ was also bringing in his equipment for the dance party.

Annabelle saw Barry putting up a backdrop for the photo booth, and Jake was checking his camera. There was even a gigantic banner that read, "Welcome to Our Annual Fall Festival."

Lila was in a corner setting up by herself. Annabelle immediately went over to see how she could be of service. When Lila saw Annabelle, she helped her sit down, took her crutches, and placed them under the table.

"I'm so glad you're here, Annabelle. My other friend Kayla couldn't make it, and I thought I would have to do all this work by myself. But you have certainly saved the day!" Lila said relieved at having extra help.

"Have no fear, Annabelle is here. And I know exactly what to do," Annabelle assured her.

Annabelle started taking all the pumpkin decorating supplies out of the box and arranging them on the table. She was doing what she loved to do, and she wouldn't have it any other way.

As time passed, Annabelle saw that everything was coming together perfectly. Everything and everyone were in their proper place.

It was finally time for the Fall Festival to begin! The music was loud and pumping. All the kids wearing creative costumes were starting to fill the gymnasium along with their families. Some of these cool costumes could definitely win the contest. Lines began forming of kids ready to play a variety of fall games, and a face painting station was also set up.

Arts and craft projects filled table after table, and plenty of food was available such as hot dogs, salty snacks, cotton candy, and juice boxes. What really made it feel like a Fall Festival were the caramel apples, candy apples, and just plain candy! Darrell and his dad brought a life-sized robot from his technology company, which was being operated by remote control. There was a long line to play with it. Kids were running all around the place.

Annabelle was just glad to be a part of this great event and happy she could still be helpful even though she had gotten hurt. Annabelle loved doing amazing things that made others happy, and this was truly one of those things. What first turned out to be a low point in Annabelle's life turned out to be pretty amazing after all.

ANNABELLE'S DISCUSSION CORNER

1. Annabelle was on the committee to plan for the Fall Festival. If you were planning a Fall Party, what are some ideas you would put together?

2. In Chapter Six, Annabelle was hurt while playing basketball. Have you ever had an accident or injury? If so, how did things turn out?

3. Kaitlyn was planning for a cool dance contest for the Fall Festival. Make a list of your favorite songs and dances.

Don't forget to read the entire Amazing Annabelle Chapter Book Series!

Amazing Annabelle—the Apple Celebration
Amazing Annabelle—the Fall Festival
Amazing Annabelle—Thank You, Veterans!
Amazing Annabelle—December Holidays and
*   Celebrations*
Amazing Annabelle—Dr. Martin Luther King Jr. Day
Amazing Annabelle—Black History Month and
*   Other Celebrations*
Amazing Annabelle—Women's History Month
Amazing Annabelle—Earth Month and
*   Animal Celebrations*
Amazing Annabelle—May Celebrations
Amazing Annabelle—Last Day of School
Amazing Annabelle—Summer Vacation

Please visit our website: amazingannabelle.com
for free teacher/student ELA resources to use in
your classroom or at home. Thank you!

ABOUT THE AUTHOR

 Linda Taylor has been teaching students for over 25 years. She enjoys connecting with students on many levels. She is also the author of the *Daring David* series published by Lightswitch Learning. She also loves writing poetry. Linda lives on Long Island, New York.

ABOUT THE ILLUSTRATOR

 Kyle Horne has a B.A. in Visual Communications from S.U.N.Y. Old Westbury College in New York. Kyle has displayed his artwork in many local libraries. He lives on Long Island, New York.